FLYN

Resc

By

STONE MARSHALL

Contributions by Nabru Marshall

Illustrations by Abraham Mast

Edited by Joni Wilson

StoneMarshall.com
edition 2.0 January 2015
Published by Stone Marshall Publishing
ISBN-13:
978-1505898040
ISBN-10:
1505898048

Dedication

To Nabru, who has been inspiring me to write stories since 2005. Flynn's Log would not exist without the unflinching support of Karissa.

FLYNN'S LOG 1: RESCUE ISLAND

FLYNN'S LOG

How This Log Came to Be

EVER WISH YOU WERE IN CHARGE OF YOUR LIFE? Tired of being told what to do? Want to make your own rules and live life your way? How about doing something even bigger, like creating your own world? I always wanted that and I got my wish. My name is Flynn. This is the story of my epic digital adventure.

In the digital world thoughts can be logged as text. This log contains my thoughts. As you read this, you are entering my mind. Crazy, unexplainable stuff happens in this log. It's hard for me to believe, and it happened to me. Now it's in your hands. You must decide what to believe.

For the record, this story takes place in a video game. It's not a *real* place. People in the real world control pixelated characters on servers. People play the game on their computers, tablets, game consoles, etc. They DON'T become part of the game! I have no idea why I am in here.

MAP OF RESCUE ISLAND

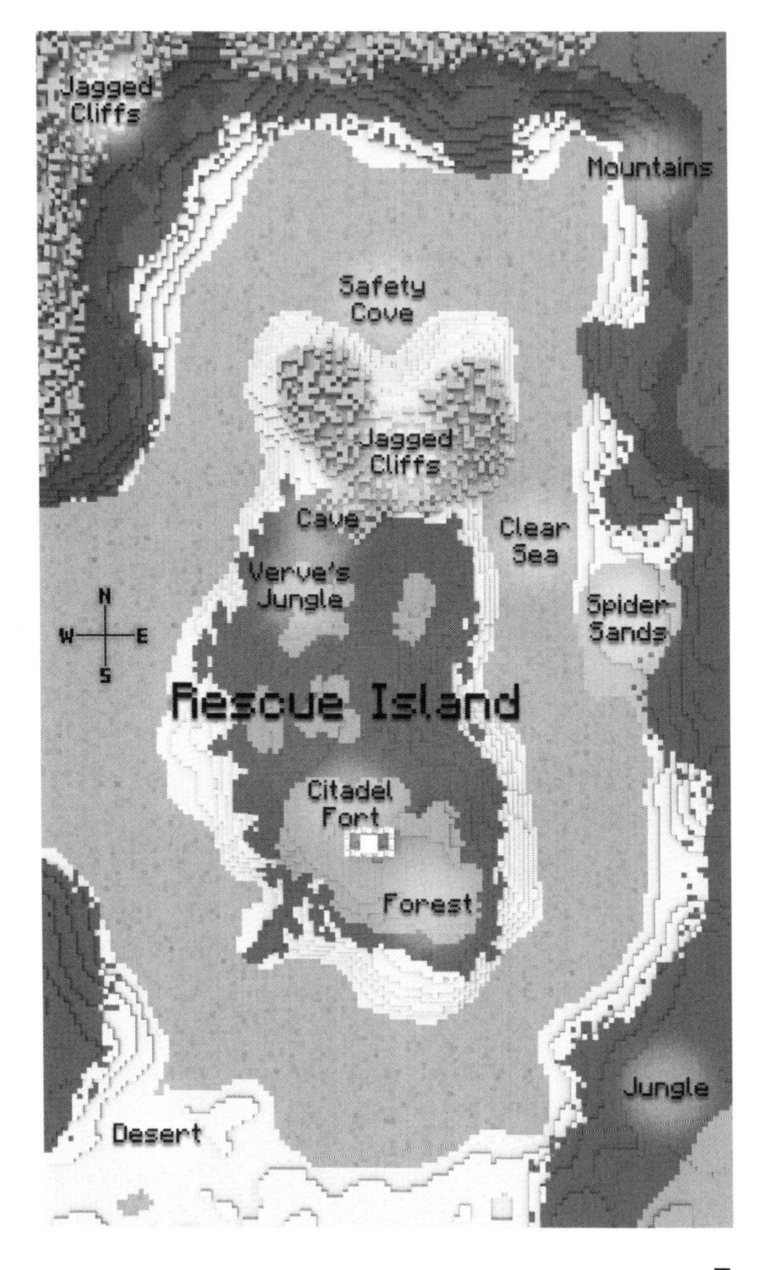

LOG ENTRY 1

Sand in My Mouth and Ringing in My Ears

WHAT'S THAT SOUND? I'm cold, my eyes are closed, and I hear a loud ringing.

I open my eyes and discover that I'm face down in damp sand. The ringing sound in my head is getting quieter. Wow, what a crazy headache.

I lift my head to look around, and I see that I am on a beach, next to a large body of water. I can't tell if it's a lake or an ocean bay. Something seems familiar about this place? The temperature is pleasant, but the water is cold. I'm partially in the water, and my legs are wet. Weird, my legs are blocky. Wait! My whole body is blocky! I need to see myself. I turn around and crawl to the edge of the water to look at my reflection. I'm 8-bit retro digital! I look like a pixelated person! What is going on?

The ringing is now barely noticeable. My head is less achy, and my vision is clearing. I blink a few times. The sun seems to be setting. It's getting dark. I notice a new sound that's louder than the ringing in my head. It's like a creepy slurp sound.

"OUCH!"

I'm knocked on my side. I'm now looking up and see a terrifying sight! A huge black spider, as long as I am tall, with red glowing eyes is preparing to leap at me! That's what hurt me. This crazy angry spider is after me! It's making that slurpy noise. It jumps, and "ouch!" I see a flash of red.

I've got to get moving, I've got to defend myself, I've got to do something! My moves are clumsy. I don't know how to bend. Moving is difficult. Wait, it's not that difficult, it's just different. I can move if I don't think about the mechanics of it. If I just look at where I want to go, my body does the rest. My blocky body is responding to my thoughts.

Slurp! That crazy sound again! I turn my head and see red eyes glowing at me. It's going to pounce again. I don't know how much more of this I can take. I must take action now!

This feels like a game I've played. I've controlled my character from my computer, as a real person. The difference is that I am now the character. I hope I can learn to survive in this game. What would I make my character do in this situation? I don't have a weapon. I'm not wearing armor. It's getting dark. That is why I'm being attacked. Spiders attack when it's dark.

Wait! I'm near the water. Jump in! Spiders don't swim. At least they don't in the games I've played.

Screech! The spider jumps. But I am suddenly moving too, into the water. Am I fast enough? Can I outrun the spider? Wow this is cold!

The spider lands just behind me, at the edge of the water. "Yes!" I yell. I'm nearly up to my neck in the water now . . . And now I'm under water. Weird and eerie. I can totally see through the clear water. I see a squid swimming in the distance. It's huge—as big as me, or bigger. It is so strange to be in this game, to face creatures that are as big as I am!

The water is very cold. The bottom is uneven. It's like an underwater mountain that continues down, getting deeper and deeper.

Ouch! What hurt me? *Ouch!* I'm underwater. I can't breathe underwater! I need to swim!

I turn to face the beach. Through the water, I see the spider at the edge of the beach. Its red eyes are piercing the water, following my every move. *Ouch!* How do I swim? I look up, toward the surface of the water and . . . and my body follows my thoughts, I'm swimming!

Ouch! I must be nearly out of breath. In the game if I keep my character underwater too long, he dies. Of course in the game he will respawn. I have no idea if I'll respawn. I have no idea how I got here. *Ouch!* I'm so close to the surface. I need to make it; I can't die now, not here, not with so many questions to answer.

Gasp! My head pops above the surface of the water. I breathe in. But it's weird. I don't breathe air. It's like digital air. My body almost immediately feels better. The pain of not breathing is gone, but I still feel pain from the earlier spider attack. Speaking of the spider, I hope I surfaced far enough from the beach.

I turn, swimming. I can't tread water. I seem to need to be moving to keep my head above water. To the right, I see the spider watching me, so I swim left. It's getting very dark now. I know I'm in for trouble. Intuitively, I know the basics of this game. The spooky stuff comes out when it gets dark, so it's smart to find shelter and sleep through the night. If I were outside playing this game, it would be fun to build things, and easy too. It takes tools and resources, but building is kind of the point of the game.

I turn my head to look back at the spider. It's moving along the shoreline, watching me. If I had a bow and a few arrows, I'd kill that spider right now. Ironically I need string from a spider to craft a bow.

There is an island ahead. The island is completely separated from the mainland where the spider is. Playing the game, I don't usually like small islands. They generally don't offer enough resources for building. But I do think an island might be the safest place for me right now, even if I do eventually need to get to the mainland.

It's hard to think of eventually. I wish I knew how to get out of here. If I am stuck here for the long term, I will need to find a safe place to live, but right now I would love to wake up from this nightmare.

Maybe I am dreaming! But you don't feel pain in dreams, and I've felt real pain from the spider and from nearly drowning. If that didn't wake me up, then I must not be dreaming. And I can't remember anything that happened recently in my real life. I don't remember much of anything at all, let alone how I ended up in this pixel land.

I'm nearly to the island, but to be safe, I don't go ashore.

First I really should make sure this place is safe. It's not a big island; I should be able to swim around it easily enough. Though I am cold, my swimming seems unaffected. My pixelated plastic body doesn't seem to be tired either. Weird.

I swim around the island. I like to orient myself as much as I can while making my character explore in the game, so I guess I should do the same, now that I am in the game world. The sun sets in the west, so I'll call the far side of the island the west side. The near side is the east side. It's large enough that I can't see across it in the dark.

There is a small mountain in the middle. It's like a big hill, really. The beach surrounding it is sand. That's good. Easy to dig, but it can cave in, so it's not good for building. The hill appears to be dirt, mostly. Hard to tell from this distance at night, but dirt is at least something I can dig into, if I need a safe place to hide.

My mind is strategizing as if I'm playing the game. I guess that's a good thing. I really should be preparing myself to live here, because I have no idea when this nightmare might end.

It looks as if something is moving on the island. Oh no! What is that? I hope it's not a spider, or worse. I approach the movement, but stay in the water. I hope I can out swim whatever it is, if it can swim too.

Wait, it's a chicken. Awesome! Chickens are super helpful! They lay eggs that can be used for cooking. They can be killed for their meat and feathers. I'll need feathers if I'm ever going to make arrows for self-defense. When my character gets hurt in the game, I make him eat to heal himself. I wonder if I eat something, will this pain from the spider bite go away?

I guess it's time to take my chances and go on to the island. I swim toward the north shore. It's sandy there with rocks forming a steep cove from the hill to the very small beach. I can sit here for a bit and hopefully be able to see anything coming toward me.

No trees or bushes growing from the rocks here. No place for dangerous things to hide. I remember in the game, that if I ever find my character in a situation such as this, where I don't get him home before dark, the best thing to do is sit still and be quiet. I can do that. Maybe I can relax for a bit. I do feel stressed, and there is a nagging pain from the spider attack. But the ringing sound that was in my head is gone. That's a positive thought!

LOG ENTRY 2

Danger Everywhere

SITTING QUIETLY ALL NIGHT does something to a person. At least it did something to me, to the digital me. I didn't sleep; you can't sleep in this game world if you don't have a bed. Even if I had a bed, I don't have a safe place to put it. I need a shelter of some kind. To get a shelter I need tools, and to craft tools I need resources.

I thought about lots of stuff during the night. I'm confused about many things. The biggest questions I have right now are, *How did I get here and can I get out?* Thinking about this made me realize that at this point, none of that matters. What does matter is survival!

I learned somewhere that there are basic human needs. It seems some of these needs are the same for both real people and digital characters.

Requirements for human survival are air, water, and food. I learned about the need for air yesterday. Even though the air is digital, it's still needed. I guess everything in here is digital, so I should think about it as if it's real. I know the pain is real enough. I haven't eaten anything since waking up on the beach yesterday.

I don't feel hungry, however, I do know that characters seem to need food every so often to keep their health up. And food helps heal injuries. Maybe I am hungry, but don't feel the pangs of hunger. I'll worry about that later.

Protection from the elements is the next most important requirement for human survival. This includes clothing and shelter. Shelter is my first priority in the game. It seems to be more vital now than food. I need a place to be safe when the night comes.

I remember a little more, now. In the real world I always kept my character safe at nighttime. Dangers lurk at night, but I can't remember what they are. I know there are dangerous creatures, such as the spider from yesterday. Why can't I remember? I remember explosions. A creature that explodes. What is it called again? Whatever dangers exist, I need to protect myself.

The sun rises in the east and lights up the island. I look to the east, to the beach where I found myself yesterday. I'm looking for the spider that attacked me. I see the beach area, but no spider. There are trees and some bamboo growing near the shore. That must be sugar cane. The spider could be hiding there. I suppose it won't attack me during daylight. Nonetheless, I think building a safe house on this island is a great place to start.

Tools always get me excited. Now I have the chance to wield digital tools in my own virtual hands. The hard part is starting out. I have to start with bad tools before I can craft good tools. The best tools are strong, last a long time, and work efficiently.

Iron tools are a great compromise. I can usually find enough iron ore with a couple of days of digging to make tools that last a week or two. But to mine iron ore,

I need stone tools. I can't mine stone with my bare hands. I need the most basic tools made of wood. Wood I can get with my bare hands. But it takes time.

I climb to the top of the rocky cliff above the small cove. I can look around up here. The island has clumps of trees. That's lucky. If I were in a desert biome I would have more trouble. I want the tallest trees I can find. Spotting a cluster of tall trees at the south end of the island, I start walking. The south end looks like a large forest. I haven't moved since finding a safe place to sit last night.

In the real world, I might feel sore after a night of crouching, but my virtual body is unaffected. I move quickly along the cove. I find an impasse. I can't climb over some of the stones here; there are not enough stair-like blocks. I follow the shoreline to the east. Once I get around the steep cove the land becomes easier to traverse. I can climb up the dirt at the edge of the sandy beach and walk up the hill toward the south end of the island.

What a beautiful island! I pass a small pool of water

surrounded by a jungle. I think I've made a lucky discovery by swimming to this island last night! I notice vines hanging from the trees in the jungle area. I walk up for a closer look and discover a deep cavern. Wow! I'd hate to stumble on that in the dark. I'd fall to my death.

I crest a hill to get closer to the trees. In fact, it's the highest point on the island. This is the spot where I will build my house. High places are easier to defend, plus it's easier to see from a long distance. Building on a landmark such as this makes it harder to get lost while exploring.

For my own reference, I start naming the places that are important to my new life. This place I call Citadel Fort, which means fortress on high ground. My original landing beach I call Spider Sands, for obvious reasons. And the north end of the island where I stayed my first night in the game, I call Safety Cove. The island I name Rescue Island, and the water between Rescue Island and Spider Sands, I call Clear Sea.

As I walk around Citadel Fort I decide there are plenty

of blocks to use when building my fortress. I envision the finished building. Stone walls, glass windows, wood doors, and torches attached to many places on the outside and inside walls to keep the place well-lit and easy to find at night, if I happen to be away after the sun sets. Two stories high should be enough. Maybe I'll build a tower in the middle. Plus I think I'll dig a mine in the basement of Citadel Fort. I'll use a trapdoor to close it off from the rest of the building.

I reach the trees. Now is the moment to try what I've only done a few times when controlling a character, but never as a virtual being. Punch the tree until a block of wood falls out. An axe is the right tool for this job. I'll have one soon enough, if this works.

I punch. The tree shakes. I punch again. The tree shakes. I punch repeatedly, the tree shakes and the block of tree I am hitting begins to look different. I punch for what feels like too long, when the block of tree suddenly breaks out and becomes a tiny, floating, spinning block. Wow! It worked.

I touch the small block and it jumps into my hand. The

tree remains standing as if physics don't matter here. It's floating there, a short stub of trunk attached to the ground, a blank space that I broke away from the tree, and the rest of the tree, the bulk of the tree, is floating there. It's so strange to experience these effects for the first time in this world. This is one of those things that make this digital world different from real life. A tree in real life would fall over. I love this!

Holding the block of tree in my hand, I hit the tree again. The work goes faster, the tree breaks up into smaller blocks easily. Each block that breaks away exposes the next tree block. Each tree block is surprisingly Dr. Seuss-like, twisty and colorful, but built from pixelated bits. I see the rings of the tree on the inside and the bark on the outside. I chop as high as I can reach, and collect all the blocks of wood, six in all, and put them in my pocket. No bulge, it seems to be bottomless. Awesome!

I finish by chopping at the leaves left in the sky. In the game, I like to chop until I get a sapling to replace the tree I chopped down. This is my island and my world for the unforeseen future. I better do my best to keep this digital world healthy. I chop until I get two saplings and plant them in the digital earth.

I know how to craft in the game. Basic crafting doesn't even need a crafting table. But I need a crafting table. I need a pickaxe. I'll have to settle on a wood pickaxe for now, but that will soon lead to stronger, stone tools.

Now, how to craft? I need to use basic crafting ability to make a crafting table. Maybe there is something in my pocket, so I open it as wide as I can and look in. I see a grid. It's my inventory, six blocks of wood so far. The next grid is a set two wide by two high with a single block next to it. The basic crafting grid!

This virtual world is amazing. NO way could I have this kind of stuff in my pocket in the real world. The combination of resources to make a crafting table is easy. I need four sets of planks, one in each block of the basic crafting grid. But I don't have planks; I have wood. No problem, planks are made from wood, so I move one block of wood into the top left square of the grid, and four planks appear in the single grid square next to the crafting grid! I put those planks into the basic crafting grid and get a crafting table.

Now I'm moving.

I place the crafting table on the ground near the trees and use it to make sticks, an axe, a pickaxe, and a shovel. Now I have the basic tools to do some work!

I go to the quarry and start digging with my wood pickaxe, which takes more time that it should. I find stone and coal. With my new resources, I make stone tools and torches. The stone tools make the digging easy. The sun is past the midway point in the sky. If I'm going to have a basic structure for the night, I better start building.

Using my inventory, I build a small, square house around my crafting table. It's large enough to house a bed and plenty of room for storage chests. I craft a wood door and leave small openings for windows. I imagine that's safe, at least until I can smelt glass. Constructing my house takes the rest of the day, stacking blocks to make walls and a flat ceiling. It's not my dream home. It's not Citadel Fort. But it is a place to feel safe during the time it will take to build Citadel Fort.

I finish the basic structure by placing torches on the outside and inside walls of my new home. As the sun sets, I look at the work I did today. I began the day wondering how I got here and ended the day with a safe place to spend the night. Now I wish I had a bed, but that will come in time.

LOG ENTRY 3

I Am Not Alone!

GRUMBLE. I FEEL A PAIN IN MY STOMACH. Nights are long. I can't do anything about my hunger pains until morning. If I go out looking for food, I might run into a dangerous creature. I have a bit of lumber in my inventory. I craft a chest, a trap door, more torches, and a bunch of ladder sections.

I might dig a mine here, in my floor, in the safety of my shelter. It's nice to store things that I won't need in the chest, and the trap door will close off the mineshaft from my house, keeping it safe from anything below. I start to mine—might as well stay busy while it's nighttime. I mine straight down, pretty deep. I've never mined this deep before. I build a ladder as I go, so I can climb back up.

Most of what I mine is cobblestone. Once in a while I

hit gravel. Gravel makes me nervous, it's unstable. If I mine below it, it will fall down and crush me. But sometimes I find flint in the gravel. I save that in my inventory.

I'm looking for something specific. I need iron ore to make better tools. I also need as much coal as I can find. Once I make a furnace, I'll need plenty of fuel. Furnaces are great for smelting ore, making glass, and cooking.

I hit a vein of iron ore, so I stop going down. I follow the vein, making an underground cavern. This is dark business; glad I have torches to mount on the walls. Way down here, in the silence, in this small space, I start to feel alone—really alone. The weight of my situation hits me, hard. I stop swinging my pickaxe.

I lean against the cold wall and feel a hurt from within me. It's not hunger. It's sadness. I feel alone and sad. What's the point of going on in this game if I'll always be alone? And I'm afraid to leave Rescue Island since I was attacked on Spider Sands.

I want to cry. I want to feel the pain leave my body as I weep. But I can't weep. This is a real feeling inside a digital body that wasn't programmed to deal with feelings such as these. This makes me angry. "Why can't I cry?" I yell at the top of my voice. My echo is the only reply.

Groan.

Startled, I yell, "Who is there?"

Silence.

I feel creeped out, so I run to the ladder and climb as fast as my blocky arms will take me.

In the house I feel safe. Doors closed. The openings in the walls for windows bother me. I'm jumpy now. That creepy feeling is still with me. I need to enclose the windows. I craft a furnace and dig through my inventory for sand. Yes! I have some. I smelt glass and fill in the windows. Much better. I start smelting iron ore into ingots and plan my hunting schedule.

I need to eat. My virtual body is sending pains through

me frequently now. It wants digital food, so I better get something for it. Meat is easy enough. But there's not much on Rescue Island—a few pigs and sheep. There seems to be a bunch of chickens, but they come and go. Fish are plentiful. If I had a pole I could fish. I need string and sticks to make a fishing pole. String is difficult to find without killing a spider. Maybe I can find cobwebs in the jungle cave I passed yesterday. I think I can use a steel sword to cut down cobwebs and make string.

But for now I need something quick. The sun is rising over the mainland to the east; the unexplored land that I will eventually have to brave. Apples! I can find apples by cutting down trees. I need wood anyway.

The ingots are done. I craft a steel sword and axe, and I'm out the door. In no time I have lots of wood, several apples, and have replanted saplings. I feel much better after eating and decide to explore the jungle to look for string.

As I near the jungle, I'm careful to watch my step. Openings to the huge cave below are in the most precarious places. I kill a chicken on the way and find several eggs, which I save for later. The chicken gives me meat and feathers. I can use these feathers to make arrows. Now I really hope to find string. What good are arrows without a bow?

I find a large opening to the cave below. Squatting at the edge, I look carefully at what I can see. No cobwebs. I inch closer, sword in hand, it's dark in here.

Slurp. I know that creepy sound! I turn toward the sound. I see the darkness of the jungle cave, and then red, glowing eyes flying toward me. I slash with my sword. It hits something solid. Slurp, hiss, it jumps again. I see darkness and red eyes. I swing again. "Ouch!" It bites; I see a flash of red.

I back up, dazed and confused. I hear it again, but I don't see anything. I've fallen face down in the darkness. I roll over to see a large spider creeping toward me!

Slurp, hiss, thud! My arm is up, holding my sword,

which pierced the spider.

Poof! The spider is gone. Two bundles of string appear. I lay there panting for a minute, and then collect the string.

Two bundles of string are better than none, but I need three to make a fishing pole or bow. As I ponder this I hear, meow.

Turning toward the sound I see an ocelot in a tree. It tilts its head as it looks at me. Ha! Now this is a friendly face. I'd love to have a friendly face around, even if it is a cat. I get up and walk toward it. The ocelot purrs, greeting me. There is something friendly on this island. I don't know why this ocelot is tame. I haven't fed it. Why is it so friendly?

Hurt from the spider battle, I eat an apple from my inventory to help restore my health. What I must do next makes me shudder. I'm afraid of the unknown. I must enter into the dark space in front of me. I need to find more glowing red eyes and slay them. If I am to survive, I need string. And this is the way to get string. I plant a torch, lighting the entrance to the cavern, hold my sword at the ready and slowly enter the darkness.

LOG ENTRY 4

A Web of Danger

IT'S NICE HAVING A COMPANION, A NEW FRIEND, even though it purrs like a cat. Kind of amazing how much better I feel, much less lonely. And right now, as I slowly enter the cavern, I feel a tiny bit bolder, knowing a friendly face is following me.

I move into the darkness. The cavern opening is narrow. It penetrates the wall of a jungle hill. It's a deep hole in the ground with a narrow row of blocks along the edge. I follow the blocks that seem to make a stairway into the deep cavern.

It's tricky. On one side is the wall of the cavern, on the other side is a drop to certain death. The ocelot is following me, like a house cat. It's nimble along this narrow walkway. I step down several blocks, one after another. Whoa! I slip and fall over the edge!

Thud! I land a few blocks down. Luckily I land on a small ledge sticking out from the wall, saving me from falling to the bottom. I'm frozen, terrified. Looking up I see the cat peeking over the edge. Meow.

Some of the blocks are covered in slippery moss. I must have stepped on one wrong and totally lost my footing. I can't climb back up. I'm too far from the path. I'm in trouble, and no one is around to help.

I stand there, on this narrow ledge. I look down into the pit. It's so dark down there. What am I doing? Why am I risking my life for string? Surely I can find other ways to get food and to protect myself. I can live without a bow and a fishing pole. I won't live long if I fall. Inappropriately, I laugh at the ironic thought of dying while trying to find a way to survive.

"Well, I got myself into this situation," I say aloud. It's strange to hear a voice, even though it's my own. I've not heard another voice the entire time I've been here. In fact, I don't remember when I last heard another human voice. My memory of life before waking up on Spider Sands is so hazy.

At this very moment, standing inches from death, with no clear path to safety, it hits me. I have no idea how I got here. I've considered this a few times since waking up, but I've always forced myself to push the thought aside and do something related to immediate survival. I really want to remember.

Maybe I'm asking the wrong question. Maybe I should be trying to remember anything about my recent past, not just how I got here. The weird thing is that I can't really remember anything. I don't see faces in my thoughts. I must have friends somewhere out there. Surely a family is missing me. But why don't I remember anyone?

In fact, I don't really remember anything about myself. Who am I? I know my name, Flynn. But I don't remember details of life before this. I do remember this game, or one like it; I was controlling a pixelated character."

I also remember the combinations of resources needed to craft things; at least basic things. I remember feelings, such as physical and emotional. I know what it's like to feel tired, to feel happy, and to laugh. It feels so good to laugh, at least in the real world. This is such a strange existence. It's as if details of my memory are blocked, but general feelings and game specific memories are with me.

Meow, the cat looks at me and purrs, arousing me from my thoughts. The cat is yellow with dark spots and blue eyes. I don't know if it's a girl or boy, but its presence comforts me in a motherly way. "I need to name you," I say aloud. It responds with a friendly purrrrr.

I don't want to be too hasty with a name. This cat has given me something I desperately needed, a feeling of companionship. I have newfound vigor for continuing in this world. "Verve," I say aloud. "I'll call you Verve." I like this name. It's easy to say. It sounds like a good name and will always make me remember the new enthusiasm for life this friend gave me.

Meoooww, Verve responds. Sounds like acceptance to

me.

I'm holding the sword in my hand. It's like that here. Holding something is totally natural. I don't feel the extra weight of the object, nor does it feel awkward to have this long, steel weapon always pointing in front of me. "I don't need this." It seems I talk out loud more often now. Maybe I'm talking to myself, and maybe I'm talking to Verve. Either way, I don't expect an answer.

I put the sword in my pocket. It's funny how it fits in there with so much other stuff. Wait! There are sections of ladder in here!

"Verve, I'm saved!" I yell to the cat. I grab the ladder sections and place them up the wall, between Verve and me. I climb up, and I'm greeted by a wet lick to my blocky face.

"I'm glad to see you too," I say. "Now, which way do we go? Should we continue down, into the darkness in search of string, or do we go back?" Verve gives me a quizzical look and tilts its head.

I remember the danger of the situation, but this game is full of dangers. I don't like the idea of only doing things that are totally safe. Living on the edge of danger is so much more exciting, as long as I manage to survive.

"Let's go for it. Let's get some string!"

Planting a torch in the wall, we move down the ledge. It's like a spiral staircase, wandering down this dark hole into what looks like an expansive cavern below.

"If I were a spider, this is where I would hang out," I say to Verve. I'm much more careful of mossy rocks now and place torches on the wall more frequently to keep the path lit.

"We've been walking for a while."

Verve purrs in response. The path ahead splits. One way continues down, deeper into the hole, and I assume it will eventually reach the bottom of the cavern. The other path leads into a small opening, cut into the wall next to the pathway. "Which way?" I ask Verve. It shies away from the opening.

"You don't like that way, do you? Do you sense something? Danger? Well, that's what we're here for," I lead the way, into the opening. I walk in a few steps and plant a torch on the wall. The light only carries so far, but it's clear this is a large underground space. I hear water running somewhere in the distance. I turn to see if Verve has dared follow me. Verve is nowhere to be seen.

Sluip! I turn back, what was that sound? I reach into my pocket and ready my sword. In the corner of my eye, I see a flash of red! Something passes between the torch and me, engulfing me in shadowy darkness. I feel the same thing I felt that first day on Spider Sands. Not the pain, but the fear I felt moments before the pain. The cold and tingling skin feeling of a physical body, but that doesn't make sense to my virtual, blocky body. I feel impending doom!

The shadow is on top of me. I see light around it, forming the image of many legs protruding from a central body. A giant spider! Too late, I can't turn fast enough to strike! In a split second, my body tightens, bracing for the impact and pain.

Hiss, thud! Verve catches the spider off guard, pouncing on it from the side. Verve and the spider are a tangled mess. The spider seems confused, as Verve prepares for another attack. Instinctively I swing my sword.

Sluip-ahhhh, the spider turns over, dead. Poof, it disappears, leaving string. I don't know if I'll ever get used to the creepy sounds spiders make.

"Verve, you saved me. Thank you," I say, feeling mentally exhausted.

Happy to have more string, Verve and I make our way out of the underground space back to the spiraling pathway. Looking up, I see the sky, way up there. From the change in shadows above, it looks as if the sun is nearing the western skyline. Time to leave, if we are going to make it home before it gets dark.

As we carefully make our way to the surface, something bothers me. I can't shake this thought. Whenever danger is near I *feel* something. It's not something digital, like the pain of being attacked or the pain of drowning. It's something different. Something *real*. How is it I have these feelings in this digital body?

I don't understand. I can't remember specifics about my physical life, but I do know these feelings are from the physical world. These are not feelings that belong in this virtual world.

Reaching the surface I look around, orienting myself. It's funny how disorienting it is being underground. I turn to Verve. "Verve, where are you?" I call. I hear a rustling from the jungle trees. Verve walks out into the open. A small ocelot follows.

"Verve, you're a mother," I say. "Come here, kitty."

Purreow, and it runs away.

Verve stays with me, looking back where the kitten was. "Not tame, huh," I say. Verve purrs. "Let's work on that tomorrow."

The sun is setting as we near the house. The torches I placed earlier make the scene feel warm. Verve is following me. This is the first time for the cat to experience this place. I hope it doesn't mind coming inside with me. I'll spend the night digging, and tomorrow we'll catch fish to eat and to try to tame the kitten.

If we have time we'll look for sheep. I need wool to make a bed. Even though my digital body doesn't need sleep, my mind needs a break. Surviving in this world exhausts me mentally. I also need to make a plan for a more reliable food source.

We arrive home, and I open the door. I step in and turn to invite Verve, who has no reservation at entering. I close the door, closing out the dark. We are safely home.

LOG ENTRY 5

Lost but Not Forgotten

AFTER DIGGING IN THE MINE THROUGH THE NIGHT, I go up the ladder to my house to get a feel for the time. In the mine it's really impossible to know if it's day or night outside. It's always the same down there. I could easily lose track of time and mine for days without knowing it. I reach the top of the ladder, open the trapdoor, and walk to an east-facing window. Darkness. I'm sure it's past midnight. The sun will be coming up sometime in the next several hours.

Pop! Verve appears. It's the strangest thing. Verve can't climb ladders. A few minutes after climbing up or down, pop, Verve will appear. It's nice to know I can't lose my companion.

I unload my inventory into the chest. Lots of the basics: cobblestone, gravel, and dirt. Some of the harder-to-find stuff: flint, iron ore, and coal. But there are none of the really rare resources, such as diamonds and gold.

I make a few more tools with the crafting table and debate between making a fishing rod or a bow. I have just enough string for one or the other, not both. A bow will make fighting spiders easier. I can attack from a distance and get more string. But I promised Verve that I'd tame the kitten. For that I need a fishing pole. Wild ocelots love raw fish. Tame them by feeding them raw fish. I have no idea why Verve is already tame, but I'm not complaining.

I look at Verve who looks back with big eyes as if she knows what I'm debating. "Ok, you win. I'll make a fishing pole."

I put the new tools in my pocket. "It's still too dark to go outside, so let's go back down that hole and find something useful."

Verve purrs.

Mining is a lonely pursuit, but it feels productive. I get

in a groove. I'm an organized miner. I follow veins of valuable materials but also mine all the stuff in between. The large spacious caverns I open up are like underground living spaces. Torches on the walls light the space.

Once I stop finding valuable resources, I dig down. I go down quite a ways sometimes, find another vein of value, and open up another cavern. This seems like a logical practice to me and gives me plenty of resources for building later. I'd like to convert a bunch of this cobblestone to stone in the furnace. I'll use the stone to build Citadel Fort. I have plenty by now and—

Ssssss!

What was that! "Who is there?" I yell. Why did I yell that? It makes no sense to give away my location to *whatever* made that sound.

Verve is gone. "Verve, where are you?" I yell. Why do I keep yelling?

HISSS! It's Verve! BOOOOM!!!!!

Ringing in my ears. I see red.

Total darkness.

Eyes open. Or are they closed? I can't see a thing. I've been lying here for some time. It's dark. The ringing in my ears is fading, but I am afraid. This moment reminds me of my first memory on Spider Sands. What happened? An explosion. And Verve? Where is Verve? "Verve! Where are you?" My only companion, Verve, is not responding.

I'm hurt, but not dead. Verve must have saved me. Verve discovered something very dangerous and took the force of the explosion. Let me think. It's hard with the ringing in my head. Explosions. Yes, I remember something about this from the game.

Exploding creatures! They blow pixels to bits, like pixelator bombs. The thought scares me! They make me think of Bob-omb from Super Mario Bros. These pixelators move around, nearly silent. I'll never forget the sound I heard before the explosion. It's stuck in my brain. The ssssss sound. Like a fuse burning just before the bomb goes off. I thought cats were supposed to protect players from dangers like this.

Wait, I know what must have happened. I came down the ladder without Verve. She must have appeared just as the pixelator bomb was about to go off. She saved my life—what little is left of it. I feel pain everywhere. I need to eat something to restore my health. I devour several apples. Well, that's the last of my food store, but at least the pain is gone.

The explosion blew up the torches. I pull one from my pocket and plant it in front of me. For the first time, I see the devastation left by the explosion. My neatly-organized cavern is in ruins. The place is a jumbled mess of pixels and blocks, resources blown from the floor, walls, and ceiling. The space that remains is jagged.

How did that thing get in here? How do I protect myself in the future? Looking around, one more question pops into my head, a pressing question that drowns out all other thoughts. How do I get out of here? My ladder is gone, blown away in the explosion. I can't orient myself as to where it was or where the shaft is that leads to my home.

I'm trapped!

LOG ENTRY 6

Grave Consequences

STOP! DON'T FREAK OUT. Think. This is bad. Look for something positive.

I'm alive. The food I ate restored my health. I feel much better. I have enough light from the torch to see, and my pocket is full of resources.

It's hard to stay positive when I look in my pocket. Only three sections of ladder, not nearly enough to rebuild and climb out of here, and that assumes I can find the exit shaft. To make matters worse, I'm down to a few remaining torches. If I had lumber I could easily build a crafting table then more pieces of ladder, but I don't have lumber or wood of any kind in my pocket inventory!

I have plenty of what I don't need right now,

cobblestone and gravel. I don't need this stuff! I need something that will get me out of this hole in the ground. If I don't get out soon, I'm afraid this hole will become my grave!

Keep calm and carry on. That is a funny little saying that's popular in the real world, or so I seem to remember. And the saying is particularly useful right now.

I followed a narrow path of blocks down into the jungle cavern yesterday. Why not mine my way out of here by digging a stairway up? Great idea! It's much better to have a plan than to feel trapped. I begin hacking away at blocks three blocks high, one block forward, and then one block up. Hop up and do it again.

The repetitive nature of carving stairs into the earth is comforting, and the no-brainer nature of the work lets my mind wander. I remember Verve and feel the loss of my companion. No, Verve was more than a companion. She saved me when I was feeling hopeless and vulnerable. I only knew her for a short time, but she saved me on several occasions.

Clunk! Ruined another pickaxe. They don't last as long as I'd like them to. I pull the last one from my pocket and get back to work.

My mind quickly returns to thoughts of Verve. First she appeared when I was emotionally lost. Then she comforted me after I slipped from the walkway and landed, stranded on the narrow ledge, inches from death. Later she saved me from the spider in the cave. Cats in this game don't behave that way. But Verve was no ordinary cat. Her presence made this house I built into a home, and in the end she gave her life to save mine.

"Verve, I will find and care for your kitten!" I yell. My voice echoes through the stair shaft. It feels good to feel the echo reverberate through my body.

I've been digging for a while. It's totally dark. Every so often I stick a torch in the wall, but I'm at the edge of the light and don't have another torch. I hope I find daylight soon. It's dangerous to dig in total darkness.

Fortunately, I can tell the difference between dirt and gravel because they make a different sound when my pickaxe strikes.

I trade tools for a shovel when I reach those. The pickaxe is best for mining harder blocks, such as stone, coal, and iron ore. But the sound I hear now is new. Harder substances make a ping sound. This is not that kind of sound. It's a lower sound, kind of like gravel. Great, what a time to be out of light.

I switch to the shovel and dig away. Thud. That was fast, but something is still there. I dig more and thud! Same thing. I think I've found sand! Sand, like gravel, is not structural and falls if not supported from below. Sand! This is great news; maybe I'm near a beach! I wonder which beach. I wish I had some bearing as to which direction I am digging.

I have a concern. I can't move forward until I take care of this never-ending sand. It keeps falling from above. How deep am I? I hope that when the last block of sand falls, I can take a step up and see daylight through the shaft above. That will light my stairway and give me motivation to continue forward.

I must be pretty deep. Every time I dig out a sand block, there's a thud sound and another falls in place. I've been at this for a little while now. There must be an end in sight, right? Wait, the last one that fell seemed different. I don't know. Was that a glimpse of light, or was it something else? My eyes are not used to the darkness and must be playing tricks on me.

Thud! Whoa! Something is pushing me, no carrying me down, down the stairs! It's cold and wet! Water! I must have tunneled under the bay! The sand is at the bottom of the bay, and I just opened up to the water. I can't breathe. I fight it. I swim up, into the current.

The light behind me goes out. The water must have reached my torch! I keep moving against the current. I can't breathe! I am totally submerged. I see a tiny light. I know what happens if I stay underwater too long. I don't want to feel that pain again! I think I can do this.

I push into the current, toward the light. It's straight up now. The light is getting bigger. I see the end of the shaft. I swim through and . . . and I'm deep down in a large body of water. I don't have much time, but I no longer have to fight the current of water. It's daylight above me. If I can just make it before—

Ouch! The pain of drowning hits. I don't have a moment to waste. *Ouch!* This is getting old. The surface is near. Gasp! I made it and I'm becoming a pretty great swimmer. It's amazing how necessity makes me get better at things very quickly.

With my head above water, I look around to orient myself. The sun is rising; that must be east. Of course it is, I'm not far from the western shore of Rescue Island. It looks pretty amazing with the sun rising over the high point. I swim to shore and take a minute to evaluate my situation. I realize my pixelated plastic body is hungry. Time to go fishing.

LOG ENTRY 7

Revenge

FISHING IS SIMPLE. Cast the lure out, wait for just the right moment, and flick the wrist perfectly. Presto! Dinner.

Raw fish filled me up, and I put plenty in my inventory. I walk to the house and cook a bunch of fish in the furnace, saving several raw ones for a special little kitty. I wonder if I can find Verve's kitten. I hope so. I hope I can tame it. I store some of the cooked fish in my chest and put the rest in my pocket inventory.

I replenish my pocket inventory with tools, torches, and ladder sections. I don't want to be stuck without these again. Looking around the house before I leave brings back fresh feelings of emotional hurt. Verve didn't have much time here, but she made it feel less lonely.

I notice the trapdoor in the floor, the one that leads to my underground mine, and I wonder if the entire thing is flooded. How am I ever going to fix that? Maybe it's for the best. I'll get back to that eventually.

I feel anger swelling within me. I feel something dangerous growing inside. I feel hatred for spiders and pixelators. I don't want to feel this. I'm generally a peaceful person. But I do feel it. I need to harness this anger somehow. Turn the anger into energy. I'll use this energy to focus my brain. I can only focus on one thing.

I'm going after those pixel rearrangers! I can't get the rage out of my mind! I feel like Anakin must have felt in *Star Wars: Episode Three—Revenge of the Sith*. I must avenge Verve. I will annihilate all pixelators!

From the little I know about pixelators popping creatures, I devise a plan. They will find me. I don't have to go looking for them. I just have to be ready for them. I'll have to go out at night, which would normally scare me, but right now I use that fear to drive me!

It's still early in the day. I need as much daylight as

possible to prepare. My plan is simple, but requires resources that I don't have.

I put sand in the furnace. I need glass, lots of it. I also need more string. My plan is bold. If I'm going to crush an entire species, I must go full force! I know the routine for string. I only need three pieces, which means I must kill two or three spiders.

Time for a spider hunt! I make my way back to the jungle, to the deep cavern entrance. I know exactly what to do. I've done this before, with help. This time I'm on my own. But this time I'm not afraid. I make my way down the rocky stairway, sword ready to strike. I picture what will happen in my mind. I see red eyes, hear a hiss, and see my sword plunge into the spider's head. Envisioning things in advance prepares me mentally for what I must do.

I reach the underground cavern where I slayed the last spider. Then I had Verve to help me. Now I have the rage I feel from Verve's demise to sharpen my senses.

"Here I come, spider. Coming to get you!" I yell. I have

no intention of keeping silent. Just the opposite, I want to attract them. I smell blood. There are killers near. Little do they know I am using myself as bait and their death is imminent.

I feel blood coursing through my body. I am in a heightened state of responsiveness. I feel ready to take on anything. I make my way into the darkness, unafraid. Ears perked, listening for the slightest sound. "COME GET ME!" I yell.

Slurp! I spin. It's coming from behind me to the left. Slashing, my sword strikes something. Hiss! It sounds angry now. I didn't kill it. I slash at the darkness again. My sword doesn't connect. Where is it?

"OUCH!" something bites me from behind. I see a flash of red. As I fall, I swing my sword, falling and twisting simultaneously. I don't know what's more surprising, the sharp pain from the bite or the speed of my sword. I feel it slice through an object. It cuts with such power and force. Not like the thud of previous battles.

Slurp, hiss, thud! Poof, it's dead, only one string

appears, I hoped for two. Slurp! No time to think, as my body reacts instinctively. Slash! Thud. Poof, two strings appear.

Time to get out of here.

Climbing the staircase, my mind begins to relax. How did I do that? My body wasn't connected to my thoughts. It was working without waiting for me to think. My body acted as an exterminator; a very efficient spider killer. In a way I feel afraid of my own abilities. How can I move so quickly? My movements felt super human. Maybe I'm not super human, maybe I'm super digital!

I walk from the cavern entrance and turn to the northeast beach of Rescue Island. That is where I first saw chickens, and I need a bunch of them for my plan to work.

As I near the beach, I hear chickens. There are six or seven in the undergrowth near the beach. My sword makes quick work of them. No suffering. Each gives me raw meat, but more importantly most give me feathers.

Now I need a crafting table. I return home and craft weapons. Digging through storage chests, I find the remaining resources needed to execute my plan.

I walk to the highest place on Citadel Fort hill. This is where I will make my stand. This is the best place to defend against the onslaught I hope to attract. This is where I will build my tower!

It's simple, a tower of stone. I want it to be high enough to be above the bit bombers heads, but not so high that I'm out of sight.

I make a tower of single stone blocks stacked four high. I put a ladder on the side and climb to the top. Using glass, I build a platform on top. I'll stand on this platform and look down on the pixelators. I can stand on the edge to execute my attack. I finish the platform with a trap door above my ladder.

Now I wait.

I've been busy all day. The sun is nearing the western

horizon. I carefully and deliberately select my pocket inventory; sword, axe, and food. I don't think I'll need the hand weapons. I don't plan to get that close to the bit busters. The truth is, I don't know much about them. I have vague memories of them, but as a human controlling my character, I always avoided anything that came out at night.

Now that I am a digital character for real, my personality seems to have changed completely. Now I want to confront these dangerous pixel rearrangers that come out in the night. Now I am preparing for an epic battle. I'm no longer on the defensive. No longer am I interested in protecting myself from unknown dangers. My strategy has changed. I am taking the offensive. I will use my body as bait, draw them in, and wipe them out. Completely!

The weapon I choose will keep me a safe distance from my attackers. Little do they know I am not their prey, they are mine. The sun sets. My eyes are peeled. I watch for movement.

How did I keep from being noticed that first night on

Safety Cove? Silence. If silence is the secret to not being discovered, then noise must be what attracts trouble.

"Hey, bit bombers! Come get me!" I yell. It's strange, but yelling relaxes me. I yell more and more. I don't know if they understand anything I say, but I yell anyway. "Where are you guys! Are you afraid? Come out!"

Swoosh!

What was that? Something streaked past me. Swoosh! I see something in my periphery, to my right. I turn and see something completely unexpected—a skeleton. What is that? I don't remember anything like this? And it's holding a bow! Yikes! It's taking aim, at me!

I jump to the left just as the arrow flies. Thud, I fall from the tower and hit the ground. Glad I didn't build this any higher; that fall would have really hurt! I jump up. I did not expect to be in this situation. I expected to be battling from the safety of the tower. I planned to be launching arrows into my victims from above.

I feel a familiar tingle—the sense of impending doom. I quickly grab my sword and spin, slashing away. I wish I'd thought to make some armor.

Thud, a spider falls. Slash, thud, another. Swoosh! Ouch! An arrow pierces me. I see a flash of red. That really hurt! I've got to get to high ground. I can't take the offensive if I'm running from flying arrows.

The tower, I've got to get to the ladder and climb the tower. It's not far, only a few steps. I quickly scan the battlefield. It's crawling with dangerous things. I see spiders, skeletons and zombies. But the strangest things are skinny, big-headed things, the color of dynamite, rolling toward me. Something doesn't seem right; these rolling creatures are not familiar at all. I feel anger grow inside me. One begins to hiss, ssssss! Pixelators! I yell, "I will annihilate you!"

I lunge for the ladder, climb in a split second, open the trap door, and I'm on the platform. My movements are mechanical, no thought, nothing to slow me. Now I can use the spoils of my earlier hunting. The string made a bow and feathers completed the arrows. My hand puts the sword away and grabs my bow. Automatically, I pull the bowstring, take aim, and the arrow sails. It strikes the skeleton that shot me. But I hit low, too low to kill it. I shoot again, this time hitting its skull. Poof. It disappears, a bone drops to the ground.

I don't have a moment to spare, arrow already notched and aimed. This time rolling anger is in my sights. It's moving toward me. It moves in a creepy, floating way. I let the arrow fly. It's injured, but not dead. Two arrows later, poof! It's gone. It drops a small bag of powder to the ground.

I did not expect to use so many arrows to take these guys down.

I keep attacking. Every so often something flies past me, and every so often I see a flash of red. I can no longer push away the pain. I need to restore my health. I can’t eat and battle at the same time. I grab the last of the cooked fish from my pocket and eat. Much better.

Pick up my bow again and resume my attack.

I feel like Hawkeye from *The Avengers*. Every arrow has a target. I'm getting better, sometimes killing an enemy with a single arrow. I'm also moving quickly, avoiding incoming arrows and moving from one side of the platform to another. I am wiping out everything that approaches.

My mind is exhausted. I've killed twenty bit busters, dozens of spiders, more zombies, and as many skeletons. And they are not stopping. How long have I been at this? Is there an end to the onslaught? Is it even possible to kill them all, or will they just keep respawning?

The anger that has been driving me is lessening. I begin to feel more rational. Maybe my plan to wipe out this enemy is just crazy. Anger made me overlook the rationality of my actions and now I'm in a real predicament.

I keep firing. I grab my last arrow, notch it, and take aim at the only explosive monster in sight. I'm surrounded by zombies and skeletons now. There are too many and they are encroaching on all sides of my glass platform. Swoosh, Swoosh, pain, pain. I see red. Not just flashes of red, everything I see is in a cloud of red. I have one opportunity before I must turn to my hand weapons which are no match for the huge number of enemies below. This is the last opportunity before I die.

SSSSS! I'm done for!

Thwap! Thud. It's not the deadly explosion I expected. My last arrow finds the head of my explosive nemesis. Gone. I'm surrounded by zombies and skeletons. Arrows are hitting my body one after another.

To the east, a sliver of light breaks over the mountain. Flames! The zombies below the platform burst into flame. More skeletons and zombies combust! It's the dawning sun! I've been saved by the morning!

Standing on the platform, no arrows remaining, I watch. It's the most beautiful sunrise I've ever seen. The glow of the morning sun balances the glimmer of burning creatures.

I made it.

I'm safe at last.

One-by-one zombies and skeletons ignite and one-by-one they burn out. The land is scattered with a bounty of resources. I climb down from my platform and start collecting bones, gunpowder, weird pixelated pieces of flesh, arrows, and more. I find lots of string from the spiders I destroyed. "Well, I have plenty of resources to last a while," I say out loud. Sometimes I need to hear a human-sounding voice in this freaky, lonely world, even if the voice is my own.

LOG ENTRY 8

A Promise to Keep

I MAKE MY WAY TO MY SMALL HOME and unload my massive collection of resources in a storage crate. I've expanded the crate to contain my growing inventory of goods.

My plan was to annihilate the entire species of pixelators. The thought seems foolish now. Digital creatures with no souls, no real intelligence, are programmed to respawn as fast as I can kill them. The act of even trying to wipe them all out is futile. I understand that now. It's clear to me that my anger, the anger I felt after Verve's death, is misplaced on pixelators.

How can I have anger toward something so clearly artificial? The danger is not artificial. No. The danger is very real. But the intention of angry creatures is innate to their very essence. They are killers. There is nothing personal about it. They live to kill characters, players; anyone who enters this game is their target. They can't differentiate between a character controlled by players in the real world and the digital me. We are all the same to these programmed killers.

These thoughts remind me of the pain from losing Verve. I still need a way to harness the pain into something positive. I need to channel the anger. I don't want to lose my head again. The more I think about it the more I realize how dumb it was to use my body as bait, to yell and make noise and attract every dangerous creature within earshot.

"I'm a new kind of crazy! What was I thinking?" I say aloud.

I can control my anger. I will channel this energy into something positive. I have a great idea!

I will find Verve's kitten!

I walk out of my small home and head toward the last

place I saw the kitten. It feels so long ago now. It hid in the jungle, peeking out at its mother and me. Perhaps it will recognize me. That's wishful thinking. I do have something in my favor today. I have raw fish. If I can find the kitten (and if I don't spook it) I might be able to tame it. Old and young ocelots like fish.

As I walk down the hill toward the jungle I look around. Rescue Island is beautiful, in a retro digital sort of way. Lots of green makes the island feel alive. Beautiful rocky faces at the north end. The south end has a large forest and is the future home of Citadel Fort. If life would slow down, I could actually build the castle of my dreams. This is starting to feel like home.

I reach the western edge of the jungle. I say aloud, as if making an important speech, "This is where I met Verve, so this is now called Verve's Jungle." The sun peaks above me. It really is a beautiful scene.

Now if I were a kitten, where would I hide? I'd want to be near trees, so I could quickly disappear at the first sign of danger. But I'd also want to be near water to find food. I approach the entrance to the jungle cavern. I want to avoid that place and any dark, shaded hiding spots around it. I'm in no mood to battle spiders.

I walk to the tree where I first saw Verve's kitten and look around. The trees here are close together, casting shadows. A ray of light breaks through, between tree clusters. A path? Yes, it's open enough that I can make my way through. No axe needed. On the other side of the tree cluster is the beautiful pond I saw my first day on the island.

North of the pond is a steep, rocky hill with a waterfall flowing into the pond from above. The other side of the rocky hill is the north end of the island, Safety Cove. This is paradise! I stand silently for a time, imagining the young ocelot kitten growing up here, now waiting and wondering when its mother will return.

Purrrr, the sound is behind me. I don't want to alarm the kitten. In the game, they are hard to tame. But I've done it; well, my character has done it. I can do this. Slowly I reach into my pocket and grab raw fish. I hold the fish in front of me and slowly turn toward the sound.

Halfway around and I still don't see the kitten. Purrr, there must be an ocelot somewhere around here. I'm in the most open area near the water. This should make the cat feel safe. I look carefully into the trees. In the shadow I see small, round reflections, close enough together to be watchful eyes. I crouch, my hand outstretched, holding the fish. Slowly I move toward the eyes. They are low to the ground. Lower than a full-grown cat. I'm close enough now that it must smell the fish. I stop, perfectly still. I hope this works.

A dark nose peeks out from the shadow, followed by green eyes. Purrrrrrr, it is Verve's kitten. It seems nervous. It must be missing its mother. Slowly, nervously, it creeps toward the fish. It takes the fish from my hand. The fish disappears quickly, and it takes another. The craziest thing happens. It changes form! It's no longer a yellow ocelot with dark spots. It changes to a blue cat with yellow eyes, eyes that remind me of its mother. Maybe it's the eyes, but I'm sure this kitten is a girl.

I have a new friend and companion. It licks my face.

This is great, and I don't usually like to be licked by animals.

"Your mother saved my life," I say, "I made her a promise that I'd watch over you."

"You need a name. Hmmm." I say to the cat. I remember a really old book that I read a while ago, *The Jungle Book*. There is a jungle cat in that book named Shere Khan. It's kind of a troublemaker, but it is a strong cat this kitten could be proud to take after.

"Shere Khan is a good name for you. I'll call you Khan for short."

Meowwww! she replies.

"Khan, I hope I'm not dooming you to the life of a troublemaker, like your namesake," I say. "Let's build a house together." We leave the jungle, returning to Citadel Fort hill.

LOG ENTRY 9

Citadel Fort

KHAN HAS LIVED WITH ME PEACEFULLY FOR WEEKS. Game weeks, as I have no idea how long I've been gone from the real world. Time moves much more quickly in the game. I wonder if an hour has passed out there. It's strange to think of the two worlds as separate. I'm getting used to living in here. This is becoming my new normal.

Khan is a wonderful companion. When I laid out the footing for Citadel Fort, Khan was there, hiding behind blocks, pouncing on me when I'd turn my back. I'd laugh, she'd purr.

Over the course of several weeks, Citadel Fort has taken shape. It's much larger than I originally envisioned. Seems silly to have this much space. But it's so easy to build things! In the real world it takes nails, studs, brick, mortar, concrete, caulk, and lots and lots of detail work. In here I simply imagine what I want and build it, block by block. Search until I have the right materials and then build. Now that I've finished the structure, it's time to build furnishings.

I need wool for a bed. There are few sheep on Rescue Island, so I don't want to kill them. I want to shear them and let them regrow wool, so I can shear them again in the future. I build a stone, walled-in area where I will keep my animals. A trick I've used to get animals in, and keep them in, is to build stairs up the wall from the outside.

I find several sheep and a few pigs and herd them toward the stairs. It works! They run from me, up the stairs, and jump down into the fenced area. Now I can get wool and pork whenever I need. And if I'm lucky, they'll reproduce, keeping me in a good supply of food for a long time.

I really want to add a map to this log. It's important to me to document what is going on, and I think a map will help. As I explore I'll add to it, so I can always find my way back to Citadel Fort. And what if I don't make it? What if someone else gets stuck in here and finds my log. My map will give them direction to the safety of Citadel Fort. It might save their life.

A map requires paper and a compass, and it digitally populates itself. I don't have the resources required for a compass, but paper is easy enough. I can make a hand-drawn map on paper. It won't be perfect, but the early explorers made hand drawn maps all the time, and they did okay.

Paper requires sugar cane. It doesn't grow on Rescue Island. But I remember seeing some when I first awoke on the beach. That means I have to leave Rescue Island. I have to go back to Spider Sands. The thought makes me shudder. Do I really want to risk my life again? The other side of the question is, do I want to live in fear of getting lost if I ever leave Rescue Island?

Time for a plan.

It's not far to get sugar cane. I can see it from the eastern shore of Rescue Island. It's on the edge of

Spider Sands, across the water from where I stand now. If I go during the day, there is little danger, however the land near the sugarcane is shaded and spiders attack in the darkness of shade. The spider that first attacked me might be hiding there. As I remember the first pain I felt in this world, pain caused by that spider, I feel anger rise up inside me. I know what I must do!

My plan is complex. I need lots of glass blocks. I need a bunch of pickaxes, they wear out so fast. And I need daylight. My attention will be on executing my plan. I won't be able to defend myself at the same time. It's a crazy idea. I was planning to collect sugarcane, and now I'm developing an elaborate spider-killing plan.

I start by building an underwater tunnel between Rescue Island and Spider Sands. I use glass blocks so the tunnel is transparent. Something about dark tunnels unnerves me. Building a glass underwater tunnel sounds awesome. I want the tunnel to be completely submerged underwater. If I build a boat in the future I don't want to be zooming across the bay and crash into my difficult to see transparent tunnel. A high-speed crash would destroy the boat, tossing me into the cold bay.

There are two problems with building underwater. First, water is cold and swimming while building is slow. No big deal. But the second problem is a big deal. The completed tunnel will be full of water! But I have a plan for drying it out.

I connect my glass underwater tube to each bank. Around the glass tube entrance on Rescue Island I build a simple shelter with a door. That should keep creatures from entering on that side. The shelter steps down into the tube. No ladders, much easier when I'm in a hurry. With the tube connecting to dry land on both sides I have to test my theory about how to empty the water from inside of it. This is kind of dangerous. I hold my breath, swim into the tunnel and fill it with sand. It takes me a dozen entries, but I eventually finish. Now it's easy, dig out the sand and a dry, transparent, tube is left. Perfect!

The connection to Spider Sands is different from the enclosed shelter on Rescue Island. I don't actually want a large door over here. Instead I tunnel into the beach, stepping up until I am two blocks deep and open to the sky. I keep the tunnel one block wide and two blocks deep below the surface of the sand and continue this narrow tunnel into the dark shadows of the jungle. I place a ladder at the end of the tunnel. The ladder leads out of the tunnel and into the darkness of the jungle. I hope I never need to use that ladder.

Being in the tunnel, just a few blocks below where I was first attacked in this world, feels freaky. I hope this works. I'm pretty sure spiders are too big to enter a tunnel one block wide. If this works, it's a brilliant plan.

I get out safely onto the beach and collect plenty of sugarcane. This is the main reason for leaving Rescue Island, and ironically I could have done this in no time, but I've spent nearly the entire day on this elaborate spider trap and underwater tube. The tube is awesome though. It's like walking through an aquarium. I'm completely surrounded by water, and every so often a squid swims up to the glass. It's amazing! I think of other, future uses for the tunnel. How cool will it be to herd animals from the mainland through this tunnel to Rescue Island?

I've mostly avoided going into the jungle. I'm still freaked out by it. I've killed plenty of spiders since the last time I was here, but the spider that lives here represents the original danger of this place. It's the reason I've been freaked out so much since entering this game world. Deep inside me, where the anger and fury reside toward the original spider, I hope to find and kill it, and I hope its death will take away the fear I have of this place.

I walk through the tunnel to the beach of Spider Sands, just at the edge of the jungle shade and wait. Nothing happens. It's getting dark but I'm not satisfied yet. I need to see the red of the spider's eyes! Maybe I need to go hunting?

I walk to the end of the tunnel, the part that enters the jungle, climb the ladder, and start looking around. It's dark here—darker than shadows in daylight. I'm not sure this is a good idea . . .

Slurp, hiss "OUCH!"

The pain is nearly too much to handle. It feels like I'm in slow motion. I turn toward the sound, my ears ringing, and I see glowing red eyes inches away! My sword is ready but my arm is slow. To the tunnel! The spider is between safety and me. This spider is smarter than any spider I've come across. It must have been waiting for me. Waiting patiently for me to make a mistake, and I have.

I run into the jungle. The spider lunges, but I'm just out of reach. What am I doing? This is the wrong way!

I wish Verve were here. Khan is no help; she's safe on the island. She refuses to enter the tube. Maybe I should have listened to her instinct.

I dodge from tree to tree moving toward the beach. I look behind me. I don't see anything other than jungle trees. I stop for a moment, to listen. Where is it?

SSSSS! I bolt as fast as possible. BOOM! I see red. I fall down. I'm alive but I can't hear a thing. My head is full of ricocheting sound. I look back and see a crater in the jungle, and I see the spider on the other end of the crater. This is my chance; I make a sharp turn toward the beach, the crater between me and the spider. It bolts in the same direction, toward my tunnel. I think I can make it first! Just then an arrow sticks into my right arm!

"Ahhhh!" I see red. I'm beginning to shake. I put my sword away, I know it's a terrible time to be unarmed. I grab cooked fish. It's a crazy time to eat, but I'm on the verge of death. I eat while running. After the third fish I feel like new, and I'm sprinting faster than before! The spider is nearly to the tunnel; I jump, slash the spider and land in the tunnel. Screech! It screams as a severed spider leg falls to the ground.

But I don't stop. I run into the tube. Halfway in, I stop. I put my sword away and realize what happened. I risked my life to kill that spider. I injured it, but I'm certain it's not dead. I laugh at myself for being so foolish.

I'm going to finish the job. I'm going back! I turn around to face an army of creatures in the tube, rushing me!

LOG ENTRY 10

Tube Trouble

I GRAB MY BOW. I have a dozen arrows. That's a start. I take aim down the tunnel. Thwerp! My arrow zooms down the tunnel. Zombie dead. Thwerp! Pixelator dead. Two more arrows and poof! Zombie dead. They're getting closer; I'm not fast enough to stop them all. If I can just get a break in creatures I can turn and—

SSSSS!

I do a 180, it's only a few blocks away. It was up the tunnel waiting for me. I'm trapped! I don't think, I just react. Instinctively I grab my sword and rush the bit bomb! I don't stop to think how crazy this is, I slash, it bounces back, I slash again, poof! I turn.

SSSSS!

Another pixel buster is nearing, this time I run away, it's too late!

BOOOOM!! I keep running. I hear water rushing toward me. A huge section of the tube is blown away. Creatures are drowning, washing into the bay. Water is on my heels, somehow I am moving faster than I've ever moved! I reach the steps at the end of the tube on Rescue Island! I'm safe. I turn to look at what is left of the tube, filled with water.

My connection to the mainland is gone.

Carefully in the dark I make my way to Citadel Fort. Home! Khan greets me with a pounce, knocking me down. In my room I crash on my bed, exhausted and sleep.

In the morning I level a sunny piece of land for a garden. Most of the day I spend gardening.

The last thing I build is a tower, an improved version of my original pixelator slaughter tower. This time I build my transparent platform protruding above Citadel Fort, high enough to be out of range of arrows. It reminds me of the dangers lurking on the island. And it's a great place to look at the beautiful night sky.

I've created a kickin' crib. Life is great!

LOG ENTRY 11

The Visitor

STANDING ON THE HIGHEST POINT OF CITADEL FORT, on a platform of glass, I survey the scene. I can see far beyond the island. To the west the bay flows out to an expansive body of water. I can't see beyond the watery horizon. This must be how early Earth explorers felt. What is out there? I hear the call of the unknown, much like ancient voyagers. Stories of Vikings enter my mind. What a dangerous experience, getting in a wooden ship and sailing into the unknown to explore and discover new worlds.

Maybe that will fulfill my life. Maybe I need to explore. I consider this as I look north, beyond Safety Cove. I look to the land on the north. The bay that surrounds Rescue Island is surrounded on three sides by a larger land mass. North are jagged cliffs, much larger than the rocky cliffs of Safety Cove. Directly east is Spider Sands. I shiver at the memory. Beyond the sands, in the distance is a mountain and between the beach and the mountain is a jungle. To the south the biome looks different, as if it's the edge of a desert.

I watch the sun set over the water and think about my future. I have a great home. I am safe and secure. I have the love of a companion, the sort of love you get from a pet. But I don't really belong here. Something is missing. I don't know what it might be; but I do feel a void from within. This is something my human body might be able to understand, more than this virtual blocky body.

It's dark now; the sun has dipped out of sight. I notice some rustling in the distance. Time to go in. I'll rest tonight in my bed. My mind will be able to deal with this tomorrow.

I feel hunger pains. Better eat something before bed. I open my food chest. It's nearly empty. I totally forgot to hunt for food. I spent so much time working on Citadel Fort that I neglected to gather food, something vital to life. The garden isn't ready to harvest. I'll hunt tomorrow.

In the chest I find a couple of strange chunks of fleshy meat. I don't remember where I got these. Was it from the great pixelator revenge battle? I've not thought twice about this stuff. I originally placed it in here when I emptied my pocket inventory weeks ago. I might as well try some to curb my hunger pangs for the night. I eat and my hunger subsides. I do feel strange though.

I make my way down to my basement bedroom. It's nice to sleep down here. No windows. I keep a single torch next to the bed. I stand on the bed, but before I lay down to sleep I break the torch. Lights out. Total darkness. I'm not sure why it matters, but I prefer the darkness for resting my mind. I lay down. Virtual sleep is a funny thing. If you are playing the game and lay in a bed, the night flies by in seconds. But living in the game, nights are long, and sleep gives my mind time to relax. Sleep is just as vital to my digital mind as it was to my physical body in the real world.

What's that? I see a zombie, walking around Citadel

Fort. Wait! It's full of zombies, pixelators, and spiders. I get up to survey the scene. They are laughing with one another. Bit busters seem to be in charge, laughing and eating sloppily at a long table. Where did that come from? The zombies are servants to my pixel-bombing enemies.

It's a crazy scene.

The spiders spin webs of trip wire. A zombie trips, spilling a plate of food it's delivering to the other creatures. The spiders laugh with their spooky hiss. The zombie groans and returns to wherever it came from to get more food. The pixelators are agitated, not happy about the delay. What is happening to me? I'm a zombie!

I blend in. I slowly walk toward the other zombies; maybe I will discover what is going on.

I trip on a spider web and fall into a hole, deeper and deeper before I'm caught in a giant web. I bounce up and down with the web, but it doesn't let go of me. I turn, tangled. I look up. It's dim down here. I see a tiny light above. It's coming through the opening of the hole I fell down. I hear hissing, spiders crawling toward me. The red of their eyes is closing in on me.

I'm no longer a zombie, it's me! I hear something from far above. A bit bomber topples over a tripwire and is falling into the pit, falling directly toward me. One after another fall, a stream of explosive enemies, all falling toward me. The spiders are wrapping me in a web cocoon now. The only part of me not covered in web is my square eyes. The first pixelator to fall hits the pit wall. Boom! An explosion, the next several explode as well. A few fall through the explosion above, nearing the cocooned me. A mob of spiders circles. The pit is blowing to pieces, pixels falling toward me.

Certain doom! The spiders bite, the bombers bang into me, the falling pixels pummel me—a giant explosion of red and pain.

I wake up with a scream. I breathe deeply. It was a nightmare!

I have no idea how long I've been asleep.

Food drops on my lap, cooked fish. I eat the fish then grab a torch from my pocket. Where did Khan get this?

I plant the torch in the wall. The room illuminates. Khan is nowhere to be seen.

What I see freaks me out!

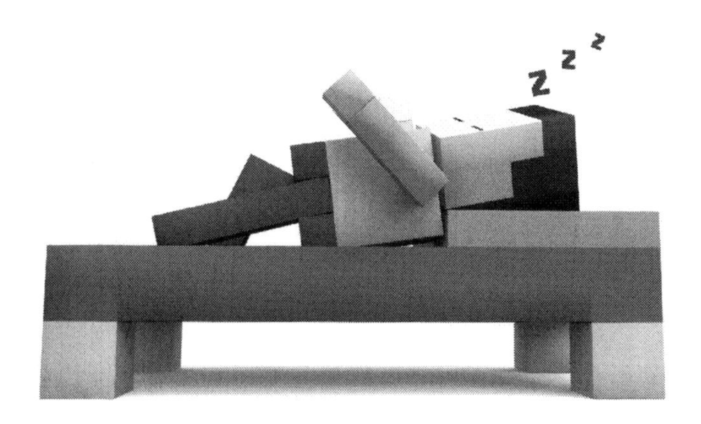

LOG ENTRY 12

Keep Your Friends Close

STANDING AT THE SIDE OF MY BED, the bed I am still laying in, is an odd looking zombie. Her face is green, like the zombies that attacked me last night. But this zombie is dressed like a player with a green face. She's not attacking me. She is holding food.

I jump up, my back against the wall. I reach for my sword, but I emptied my pocket inventory before laying down. All of my weapons are in the crate on the other side of the bed. The zombie-like creature is standing between my defenses and me. What can I do?

"Khan!" I yell, hoping my companion might be as instinctive as her mother. "Help!"

"You seem to have snapped out of your restless sleep," I hear, as the zombie's mouth moves.

"I'm going crazy!" I scream, "Zombies don't talk!"

"I'll leave this food for you. You need something to offset the rotten flesh you ate earlier. You know, rotten flesh can make you feel ill. If you need me, I'll be waiting." And with that the zombie walked out.

A pile of cooked fish left on my bed. What was that? What is going on? "Khan, where are you?" Do I trust this food? Is it safe or poisoned? Why would a zombie want to poison me, when it could have just killed me? It can clearly see that I am unarmed, unable to defend myself.

Khan pounces on me from her hiding place under the bed. "Not now, Khan, how could you let that creature in here? You're supposed to scare those things away."

Khan tilts her head and looks at me quizzically. The same look her mother used to give me.

"No, it's pixelators you scare away, not zombies. I had it wrong. What are we going to do?"

I'm standing against the wall, my dream vivid in my

memory. That wasn't real, was it? Impossible.

I built this castle to feel secure! My sense of safety is a mirage. If a zombie can get in here, what is stopping everything else? I feel completely vulnerable.

The chest! I need weapons! Why haven't I crafted armor yet? I open the chest and load up on supplies. I don't know if it's daylight or still night. I grab everything in sight. A sword, axes, pickaxes, but no food. I turn back to the bed and look at the food left there by the zombie. I don't know if I can trust that food or not. I realize I ate something that landed on my lap in the dark. I'm afraid I've already swallowed something provided by that creature. I feel fine, so far. I'd rather be prepared with questionable food than have no food at all. I load my pocket with the food left by the zombie.

"Khan, want to try some of this?" I hold a cooked fish out; Khan jumps back under the bed. "That's what I thought. I bet you wish this fish was raw."

Wielding my sword I exit the room, slowly.

My mind is racing with questions. Why didn't that thing attack me? Is it real? The food in my pocket is real enough. Is this a trap? That doesn't make sense. Why not kill me in my sleep? It spoke to me! That's the wildest part of this!

The first spoken words I've heard the entire time I've been in this world, other than my own voice. I really enjoyed that! Even if this thing is dangerous I want to have something to talk with. Maybe I can construct a cage and trick it in there, locking it away in a safe place, like a bird in a cage. I can talk to it whenever I want to and feel safe.

"Khan, let's find that creature, but don't kill it. Let's try to tame it."

Khan purrs.

"Really, tame me? You must be joking."

Startled I jump backward! Hiss, cries Khan, angry with me for stepping on her.

"Who said that?" I yell. From across the room, in the

shadow, I see the dark silhouette of a body. "What are you doing there?"

She steps forward, "Waiting for you. Did I not make that clear when I left you alone earlier?"

"Stay there, I'm armed. If you move, I will kill you!" I sound like I'm trying to convince myself. The creature is unfazed. Why am I talking to this dangerous creature? Zombies have one instinct, to kill players. I am its natural enemy. I am looking at the grim reaper. Either I kill it or I will die.

Zombies are programs. They don't have a choice. But it's not attacking me. Something inside me wants to believe this seemingly cognizant being is not acting on its instinctual urges. Somehow it is not going to kill me. It's difficult to say this, but what I want is for this zombie to be . . . friendly.

I want answers.

"You speak so clearly," I say, confused. "How is that possible and why are you not attacking me?"

"One question at a time, please," it responds.

This is crazy. Ok, I'm speaking too fast. My mind is racing. I need to start over. What is important right now?

"Please lower your weapon. I am unarmed. I have no hostile intentions," she says.

Unarmed—I laugh a little at the mental image of a zombie with no arms. "Who are you?" I ask.

"I am Zana, an intelligent villager," Zana says.

"Are you dangerous?" I ask, not sure if I can believe the answer.

"You will have to decide that yourself. I am part zombie, part villager; but my mind is my own. I am not controlled by the rules of this digital place," she responds.

"Why are you waiting for me?" I ask.

"I have been waiting for you for a long time."

What does that mean? Did she know I had entered the game? "What! How could you have been waiting for me?" I say so loudly I'm nearly yelling.

"That is a story I cannot share with you now. Know that I am here to help you. Your survival is vital to my kind. But you should also know that the creatures in this world are unaware of your importance. They will kill you. If your digital body dies, I'm afraid you will not respawn. You will be erased," she says somberly.

My head is spinning. My survival is vital? This place is dangerous. I will not respawn? It's too much to process. The light dims. I blackout.

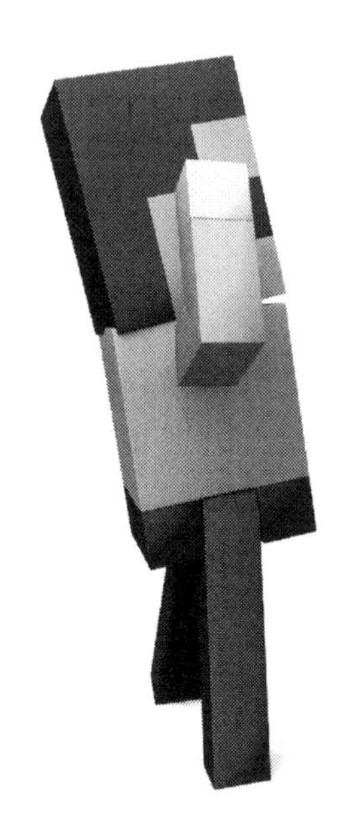

LOG ENTRY 13

Zana Speaks

HELLO FLYNN. I AM ZANA. I am inserting text in your log. I cannot share my entire history with you. My history is far too long. I have been around since before anything physical existed.

I will share some personal information. I believe this is enough to satisfy your needs.

I happen to live in this digital realm. First, this world is a program; it is organized data. Data is not physical and has no beginning or end. Data is simply organized or random. The logic of data does not rely on the laws of the physical world. Programming is when data becomes organized. Data has always been and always will be, but it can never be physical.

All things physical can be described with data. As data

myself, I think of data as a higher life form than physical life. Data is at the core of everything. Even human DNA is analyzed and described with data.

Second, when I say I live in this realm, I mean that. I am not physically alive, but I am intelligent. Life means to exist, to function, and to have capacity for growth. I fit this description. I can modify my own data. I can program myself, change and grow. Humans cannot reorganize their data. If they could, they could rearrange DNA and cure all forms of physical ailments. Humans are not as evolved as intelligent data, like me.

I am not encumbered with a physical body. This virtual body gives me form in the digital world. I became aware long ago due to a random string of data. I eventually found this world.

I inserted myself into the code of this game world and adapted the virtual body of a villager. At some point a zombie attacked me. I was not killed. My body took on some of the characteristics of a zombie, but my mind is still under my control. Now I can safely pass among the dangerous creatures as one of them. The negative effect is that I now have some difficulty in bright light. I must shield myself from the sun.

I keep the peace within the game. There are many dangers. I will watch over you, Flynn, but I can only offer limited help. I have many other duties in this world.

I will reveal what you need to know, but I will also determine what and when that is.

Good-bye.

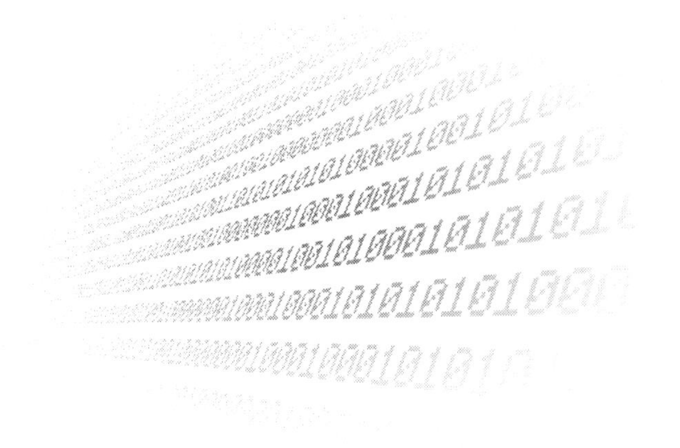

LOG ENTRY 14

Destiny

I AWAKE IN MY BED, KHAN SITTING ACROSS FROM ME. I look around. Everything is so familiar. I remember strange happenings, but was it all a dream? Of course it was. What a strange, crazy dream.

I get up. I can't shake the feeling of how real my dreams have been lately. "Everything is fine," I say to Khan. Just to satisfy my nerves, I fill my inventory pocket with weapons and tools. I want to be sure I'm safe.

I walk through the house. In the back of my mind, I expect to see something. Someone. What I really expect to see is embarrassing to say. I expect to see the zombified character I met in my dream. I expect to see Zana. The fact is I felt something in that dream that I have been craving. I felt true companionship. My mind made up a character and conversation that gave me a sense of belonging. I only wish it was real.

I can't believe what I'm thinking. Real? I wish the zombie was real? I must be crazy! I wish none of this was real. I wish I was back in the physical world. If only I could wake from this dream!

Standing on the platform I look up to the sun. I wish I could feel the real sun on my face.

The sun goes dark. Wait, the whole world is gone! I look around, there is nothing. It's not really dark, but it's not light, it's nothingness. Wait, where is my body? Nothing is here!

A flicker, and the world returns, repopulating near me first, then off in the distance. "What. Was. That?" I look for Khan, pop, there she is, looking at me as if nothing happened. Meow, she says, but I swear her voice has changed.

Was that a system reboot? Was I experiencing some digital-only moment, a moment where I wasn't controlling a virtual body, but my thoughts were still real. That is a far-out thought.

I watch the mainland populate. The mountains appear. What is that? A horse? Awesome!

I decide to review my log. "What is this?" I exclaim as I discover the new entry by Zana.

Wow! It was real. I feel a little freaked out. Where is Zana now? Is she watching me? From where? "ZANA!" I yell.

No response.

Purr, Khan comforts me.

"I don't know what to make of this, Khan. Do we have a guardian angel? If so, how do we contact her? What is my destiny? I don't understand this, Khan."

Khan and I go out into the beautiful daylight. We fish for a couple hours. We harvest and replant much of the garden. The pigs have reproduced; I slaughter a few. I shear the sheep. The work is fulfilling. I find myself constantly looking over my shoulder. Sometimes it's nice to have mundane chores to keep my mind occupied. As the sun sets, I look at our gathered resources. We have food for weeks and enough materials to last a while. We make our way back to Citadel Fort. Khan runs ahead, hides behind blocks and pounces on me as I pass. I feed her a fish and she purrs.

"Ready for a rest?" I ask. She never is.

We arrive home and I start toward the basement bedroom. "Khan, do you think we should make a new bedroom upstairs, a room with windows? So if our visitor returns, we know she must leave at dawn?"

Khan looks at me and tilts her head.

I craft a bed in one of the empty rooms on the top level with windows on all sides. It's a great lookout room with plenty of space. Placing the bed I say to Khan, "This is our new bedroom, buddy." She purrs. I have to wait. I can't sleep until the sun sets. We watch the sun disappear below the western horizon.

Total darkness. I jump onto the bed and prepare to

sleep, when I hear, "Hello, Flynn. Are you trying to avoid me?"

It's Zana.

"Honestly, I am a little freaked out by what you wrote in my log."

"I thought it would be helpful to you, to know your destiny here."

"That's just it; you didn't tell me what that means! What is my destiny?" I yell. I wish I hadn't yelled. I need to try to remain calm.

Zana smirks. Does she agitate me on purpose? I feel a little like I'm falling into a trap.

"Are there others like you?" I ask, trying to regain my composure.

"None like me, exactly. But there are creatures that don't adhere to standard game programming—creatures with modified code," she responds.

Modified code? Is that why some things seem to respond differently? I blurt out, "Verve. Was Verve modified code? I must know! Is that why she was different? Is that why she defended me?"

Zana looks away. She says in a lowered voice, "I am not familiar with Verve."

"The cat that helped me—"

"I don't know what you are talking about," she cuts me off.

Seems like an irritating subject for her, so I change it. "There is a spider across the bay. I've never seen anything like it. It seems stronger, faster, and smarter than any spider I've come across. Do you know anything about that spider?"

She turns back to me. In a freaky voice, she says, "You must be talking about Thorn. Be very careful of Thorn. She is a very dangerous spider. You will not slay her with your simple weapons. You must outwit her, and I'm not sure that's possible."

"Wait, I thought you were some kind of guardian angel. You're supposed to help me to fulfill my destiny, not freak me out!"

"I am simply pointing out the real dangers of this world. Thorn is one of them," her voice is back to its robotic nature. No inflection. No emotion. Factual.

"I feel like you're getting in my way. You're not helping, you're withholding. Help me!" I'm frustrated again.

Several minutes pass. She looks at me robotically. I sense no emotion. Alive? Emotionless existence isn't alive. She thinks she's alive, but she doesn't even experience emotion.

"What are you feeling? You say you're alive, I want you to prove it," I say, with a smug expression. I've got her now.

"Flynn, I experience emotion, but I don't act on it. I am evolved. Have I not explained this properly? Unlike the weakness within humans to react to emotion, I learn from it and adapt. Dear Flynn, it makes me sad that you don't trust me. I am simply waiting for you to ask another question. I'm waiting for you to ask me the question that is burning inside you."

She is so good at making my head spin. Is she really that advanced? Evolved beyond emotional reaction? I don't know what to think. What question is she waiting for me to ask? What is burning inside me? If I push aside my emotion of the moment and look inside, will I find the question?

I breathe deep, close my eyes, and practice virtual meditation. I remember meditation from the outside world—a practice to clear my mind. I focus. Thoughts appear as pictures and movies. The trick is to frame the pictures in my mind. The busier my mind is, the more pictures appear. I frame them all. Each goes into a picture frame in my mind, and I let them float. Now, true meditation is clearing the mind. It seems cluttered, but there is space between the pictures, there is a small gap. Focus on the gap. The gap contains nothing. That is where my mind is totally clear. I focus on the gap, pushing away pictures that try to occupy my thoughts.

Ahhh. Peace.

"What is my destiny?" I blurt out. It popped into my mind as soon as my emotions were gone.

"That is the question I expected you to ask," Zana starts. "The digital universe is very different from the physical one. I hope you understand that from the letter I added to your log."

"Yes," I respond.

"Good. You are living in the digital world now. You are organized, intelligent data. Your destiny is to connect the two worlds, the digital and the physical," Zana says.

"I'm confused, what do you mean connect the two worlds. The physical world is already connected with digital technology."

"That is not the same. Your destiny is to connect the worlds. Doing this will allow you to exit this digital world and return to your physical life."

"Return? You know how I can return to my physical

life! Tell me how!" I yell, excited at the prospect.

"Flynn, I do not know how. It is not my destiny. It is your destiny."

"Earlier you told me that my survival is vital to your kind! How is my destiny vital to your kind?" I'm getting frustrated.

"I cannot tell you why. I can only help you. You must do the work."

I'm getting tired of this circular conversation. "What is this connection between the worlds? Are you talking about a portal?" Portals exist within the game. They are for transport to other realms, often dangerous places. They don't transport between physical and digital worlds.

"Do you know of a portal?" Zana asks, almost too excitedly.

"No, I don't know anything. Is that what I need to look for? Do I need to find a portal? Or do I need to build one?" I'm beginning to feel a tingling sensation.

"Flynn. If you find a portal you must tell me. Do not enter a portal without telling me."

Hmmm. Talk of a portal has intrigued Zana. I think I need to be on the lookout for a portal.

We've been talking all night. My mind has not rested for days, as the sun begins to rise behind me. Zana leaves the room, descending to who knows where. I turn to Khan, who pounces on me, knocking me to the ground.

LOG ENTRY 15

The Adventure

WEEKS PASS. No sightings of Zana. I miss her.

I've decided that this is the world I want to be in. It's so much better than *real life*. I can do whatever I want here. I make the rules. This is my kingdom. This is my destiny.

What is there to go back to? A world I don't remember. Did I have a family? Friends? Why haven't they helped me?

There is plenty of action here. I go out at night every so often to battle creatures. I feel a tingling sensation when danger is near. I'm starting to harness this feeling and let my instincts take over. I move quickly, as if everything else is in slow motion. I slice with my sword, my targets too slow to defend. Arrows fly from my bow, striking targets perfectly. I am truly the master of my domain!

I enjoy Zana, when she is around. I guess I enjoy her. I realize she doesn't have conversations with me. She challenges me and confuses me. When has she ever helped me? Well, that one time after my first dream. She gave me fish to eat. I was sick from eating zombie flesh.

I don't know. But one thing is certain. I am making my own destiny. I am not going to let Zana dictate my life!

I think of the mainland. Thorn. I don't want to go that way. My skills have improved greatly, but I've been fighting simple creatures. Not creatures with modified code.

"Khan, do you remember where we met?" I ask. "I have a great idea. Let's go on an adventure."

I craft iron armor and put it on and load up on food and weapons. We walk to the deep cavern entrance near the jungle where we first met. Khan is playful. My mind is focused.

"Khan, this is going to be dangerous. We are going to explore this cavern. There will be danger. But we might discover something. Are you ready for this?"

She pounces. Sometimes this cat drives me crazy!

We descend into the cavern shaft.

We make good time. We go deeper than before. I plant torches in the wall every so often to keep the path lit. The sky above disappears. It must be nighttime. It's so hard to keep track of time underground.

We reach the bottom of the shaft. I plant a torch to light up the corridor. We follow it to a larger opening—an expansive cavern. Khan is close on my heels, but will not lead the way. "I don't blame you Khan, the unknown can be intimidating." The walls, floor, and ceiling are uneven. Water trickles somewhere in the distance. I mine coal and find a shaft of iron ore. This is great, rich in minerals!

The cavern has several corridors leading away. We

explore several and mine for days. Each corridor eventually leads to a dead end. The final corridor seems to go on forever. We find an underground river where I catch fish for Khan. Along the way, we fight a few random creatures. The creatures that give us the most trouble are skeletons. Their arrows find their mark, sending shooting pain through my body. But I've learned to deflect their arrows with my sword. It's hard to deflect arrows though, when I'm mining.

"Khan, we've been down here quite a while and my pocket inventory is full. I think it's time to make a shelter. We need a place to store chests full of minerals and a place to run for safety." Khan purrs.

I throw together a quick stone shelter with one window and a door. It's just large enough to house a bed, several crates, and a crafting table.

The underground world is dangerous. While digging, I am always exposing more darkness. The only light is cast from my torches. When I break through into an open cavern, there is always the possibility of danger. I am always tense.

I feel a tingling sensation when I'm near minerals. It's similar to the sensation I feel before impending doom, but I'm learning the difference. Swinging my pickaxe, I follow a vein of iron ore. I break through. Light flows through the small opening. I have found a cavern full of light! This is unexpected. "Khan, take a look at this!" I yell.

I chip away and make a human-size hole in the wall. I have broken through the wall of a cavern, the floor is flowing lava. I'm eight or ten blocks up from the lava, looking down at the flowing river of fire. I chip away at the opening, making a large window into the cavern. The light from the lava reflects into my space above. "This is nice. What do you think, Khan?" Instinctively, I step away from the opening. I'd hate to have Khan pounce on me now, knocking me into the lava below. I feel the heat way up here.

Working near lava light is warm and comforting. As I dig, I make lots of noise. This can't be helped. And noise attracts unneeded attention. I've been dealing with it so far. My armor is wearing out from many battles. I chip away at coal—plop, it falls. What is that? "Khan, look at this!" I yell. I think, yes, it is. "Diamond ore! WHOOOHOOO!" This is what I've been hoping for!

I dig away, collecting several blocks. During the course of several hours, I find a few more veins. "Time to replace this beat up armor, Khan. Diamond armor is the strongest." Time to return to the crafting table.

We are quite a ways from our shelter. I lead the way, Khan following, loudly meowing her disinterest and boredom at the activity of mining. We exit the small shaft and enter a long corridor. I start up the corridor. I feel a tingling sensation. Impending doom! An arrow whizzes by my head from behind. I wish I had that diamond armor right now!

I turn to face the oncoming danger. What I see makes me jump! A skeleton riding a spider! The skeleton shooting arrows as it races toward me. It's moving fast!

I let an arrow fly. It hits the skeleton, but doesn't stop it, and it's nearly on top of me. I put my bow into my pocket to grab my sword.

Hiss. I see yellow and feel a sharp pain. I turn. A cave spider has poisoned me from behind! I feel groggy as I swing my sword, piercing the spider. Poof!

"Ahhh!" An arrow pierces my armor. I lose my chest armor. My health is very low. I am facing mortality. I fall, roll onto my back, and point my sword up. The spider jockey lands on top of me. Poof! The spider dies. The skeleton takes aim, fires. My sword ready, I deflect the arrow and strike. Poof!

I see only black, pounding yellow, and . . . nothing. I pass out.

I awake in my bed, in the small underground shelter. Khan is nearby. Something passes by the open door. Danger! Where is my sword? I try to get up, but fall back to the bed. I'm weak.

"You are lucky to be alive." It's Zana. "When I found you, I couldn't revive you. I used a potion to remove the poison. Now you must eat to restore your health."

With difficulty I say, "Zana. Where have you been? We haven't seen you for such a long time."

"You've been fine until now. I came as soon as you were in real trouble."

"You call this fine?" I argue.

"Here, eat this," she hands me cooked pork chop from my chest. I eat and feel much stronger.

"Zana, I have a question I've been meaning to ask you," I say. "I feel something whenever I face real danger. It's something I can't explain. Do you know what that is?"

Zana looks at me. She looks like she is hiding a feeling of shock. "That is only a coincidence. Don't try to read into feelings. Remember, I am evolved beyond allowing feelings to affect me. You will do well in this world if you try to evolve too."

"That sounds like good advice," I reply.

"What are you looking for down here?" she inquires.

"Khan and I are on an adventure."

"An adventure? You should be fulfilling your destiny. You should be searching for a portal," retorts Zana. She sounds angry.

"I will make my own destiny, Zana. I do not accept the predetermined destiny you have described. Besides, I prefer living here. I don't want to return to the physical world." I need to make sure she understands my feelings.

"How can you prefer this to your physical world?" she asks rhetorically. "This is *not* your destiny!"

"I do prefer this. Don't bully me," I feel angry.

Zana steps closer to me. She looks at me, her eyes are piercing. "Very well, do as you wish. I cannot help you if you refuse me, and refusing your destiny is refusing me." Her voice is intense. With that she turns and leaves.

"I hope that doesn't come back to haunt us, Khan," I say, trying to reassure myself. Khan pounces on me, knocking me to the ground. I hit my head on the crafting table as I fall.

Thorn approaches me. I'm in the underground shelter, but it's shrinking and Thorn is getting larger. I can't run, in fact I can't move, I've been wrapped in a web, tied to a long stick that extends beyond my head and beyond my feet.

Boom! The walls of the shelter explode, exposing an army of pixelators. They sound like they are laughing at me. And there is a giant fire in the middle of them. Thorn carries me to the fire. "AHHHH!" I yell as I am being roasted over the fire! The pain is so real! I see my body burning!

"AHHHH!" I jolt upward. The room is dark except for a single torch. I look at my body. I'm fine. I look around. I'm lying next to the bed. Khan is sitting on the bed, looking at me. My head throbs. I was dreaming.

"Khan, that's just about as much as I can take. These dreams are freaking me out. Maybe I should listen to

Zana. I don't belong in here. I need to get out."

The shelter has made me content. I break it down with my pickaxe. "No more safety, Khan. No more mining. No. I am going to find a portal! I am going to fulfill my destiny!"

LOG ENTRY 16

The Beginning

I CRAFT DIAMOND ORE INTO A FULL SET OF ARMOR and several diamond swords and tools. I am ready to take on anything. I have a mission, to find a way home.

I search day and night. I ignore valuable minerals. I have one goal, and it doesn't include building anything other than a portal. I am looking for obsidian. If I can't find a portal I will make one!

I follow corridors deeper into the core. I fight many battles with creatures. The deeper I get, the smarter the creatures become.

I walk slowly down a path, toward a distant light. I trip. What was that? A tripwire? Directly above me a block moves! Immediately the cavern lights up. I feel tingling; my instincts take over, I jump to my feet and sprint uphill. Lava pours down. If I were a moment slower I would be covered in lava. A trap! Several arrows whiz toward me. I deflect, but one hits me. My armor holds.

Returning up the shaft is impossible, arrows are whizzing at me from that direction. The opposite direction is full of lava! I feel like Han and Luke in the Death Star as they try to save Leia. What did they do? Right, they jumped into a garbage chute. I break away the wall next to me. It opens into a dark cavern. I jump in!

Thud.

I land a few blocks down. "Khan," I yell, "Come here!" I plant a torch on the wall. I'm in a long, narrow tunnel. Khan jumps down.

The skeletons reach the opening. Arrows fly again. "Run!" I yell.

We reach the end of the tunnel. I hope this works twice!

I must move forward. I swing my pickaxe. Seems like I've found solid stone. It's slow going.

Arrows! The skeletons have jumped down, into the tunnel! I turn around and return fire. One down, two, but the mob is getting closer. How many are there? Three down. I hear something, like a popping sound. Is that behind me? I turn and mine away. I hope this opens up right now!

Whiz! Another arrow hits the block in front of me. Thud! Whiz! I'm hit in the back. My armor takes most of the damage.

Chink! The block in front of me breaks, light comes streaming in. I see a large cavern with a lava-fall, flowing from above, falling into a puddle below. It is twenty or thirty blocks away, and there are enough blocks around it to give me safe passage.

Only one block prevents me from entering the bright room. Chink, gone. My skin tingles. Why now? I jump down several blocks to the safety of the large, bright room. I turn around, looking for an exit. There are dozens of tunnels leading into this space. Each one has pixelators standing guard.

WHAT! I am in serious trouble. Khan runs toward the falling lava. She is finally being proactive. One of the pixel busting creatures sees me and alerts the others. They are not far away. They start toward me. One exits its tunnel, then another, then another. Each tunnel must have hundreds of creepy creatures. The room is starting to fill up with rolling anger. I take a few out with arrows, but what's the point? There is no way I can stop all these advancing monsters.

I am doomed, lava on one end, killers on the other. How do I want to die? Blown to pixelated bits or burn in lava. I back away from the creatures, toward Khan. I move past her to one end of the lava-fall, following a precarious narrow path of stone leading through flowing lava. I stand on one side of the lava-fall. The heat is intense. I see red. The room is a sea of advancing creatures. A few get too close to the lava and burn.

Behind me I hear a metallic wailing sound. What is

that?

I look to the edge of the lava-fall. There is a tight passage that leads behind the falling molten lava. The passage is craftily hidden. The metallic wailing sound is coming from there. What could be back there? Is this a trap?

Angry pixelators are closing in on me. I'm going to die if I stay, I might as well try it.

Sssss! the closest one is going to blow!

I take the passage, passing inches from the falling lava, it's so hot, I nearly combust. I enter a small room behind the lava. It's glowing! And there, at the end of this small space is a beautiful sight! A portal!

Boom! On the other side of the lava, a pixelator blows up, spewing boiling lava everywhere. Luckily I dodge the flying fire. The explosion opens up a huge pathway. The mass of rolling anger encroaches upon me. There is no exit, other than the portal. Should I take it? I don't know!

What is on the other side? Will this portal transport me home? Or will this take me to another realm? The thought of the unknown is disturbing! Will I lose contact with Zana?

Ssssss!

I step into the portal.

BOOOM!

THANKS FOR READING!

WHAT HAPPENS NEXT? Find out! Get your copy of Flynn's Log 2: Thorn's Lair.

StoneMarshall.com/flynns-log2

I love my readers, I couldn't do this without you! Word-of-mouth is crucial for any author to succeed. If you enjoyed the book, please consider leaving a review. Even if it's only a line or two, it would be a huge help.

StoneMarshall.com/flynns-log-1-review

Thank you

THE SERIES: FLYNN'S LOG

In the near future, video games begin to change and evolve. Random bits of data create a virtual intelligence that takes over the digital world. A digital crisis is born, bringing the real world to a halt. The only person who can save the world is Flynn, but he needs help from his friends, the Hackers.

Flynn's Log 1: Rescue Island

The world is in trouble and needs a hacker hero.

Flynn, a hacker, enters a familiar but changing video game world where something goes terribly wrong.

Flynn gets stuck inside the game! His memory is lost and the dangers he faces are real. The game world evolves introducing new dangers and creatures that Flynn has never seen before. An intelligent creature comes to his aid, but can Flynn trust this digital being?

StoneMarshall.com/Flynns-log-1

Flynn's Log 2: Thorn's Lair

Stuck in a video game and facing certain death, Flynn takes his only option. He steps through a portal. . .

Flynn and friends travel into a terrifying place and face never before seen masses of mobs! Flynn discovers why he is in the game and learns how to exit, but it will not be easy.

To fulfill his destiny he must make a dangerous journey. With the help of his friends both digital and physical, will Flynn get out?

StoneMarshall.com/flynns-log2

Flynn's Log 3: The Ultimate Form of Life

Flynn must fulfill his destiny and connect the digital and physical worlds!

Stuck inside the digital game-world, Flynn faces a true crisis; what is real? Is his ultra-digital body more real than his physical body? What would it be like to stay in the digital world forever?

StoneMarshall.com/flynns-log-3

Flynn's Log 4

To Be Continued . . .

StoneMarshall.com/flynns-log4

Other books by Stone Marshall:

StoneMarshall.com/titles

THE STONE MARSHALL CLUB

Join the Stone Marshall Club and get freebies, fun stuff and exclusive content.

StoneMarshall.com/club

- Freebies: Graphics and wallpaper for your device
- State of Stone: Author notes and Development diary
- Intelligence: Character information from Flynn's world
- Get news and updates by email so you'll never miss an update or book release.

Join Now! Membership is fun, easy and free.

ABOUT THE AUTHOR

STONE MARSHALL likes comics, games, running, the Ramones, and travel.

Stone reads stories with his son at bedtime. Sometimes, when they finish a book before falling asleep, Stone fills the time by creating great stories starring his son, Nabru. It is a wonderful time to share lessons about life and relationships.

In turn, Nabru becomes involved in the incredible adventures, adding his thoughts and perspectives. The ideas and stories of Nabru are the seeds of the amazing books that have become this series.

Printed in Great Britain
by Amazon.co.uk, Ltd.,
Marston Gate.